MW01119819

No Guns for Me!
Activity Book

Say No to Guns and Violence

By Q. L. Pearce
Illustrated by Larry Nolte

Lowell House
Juvenile
Los Angeles

CONTEMPORARY BOOKS
Chicago

About the Center to Prevent Handgun Violence

No guns for Me! has been reviewed and endorsed by the Center to Prevent Handgun Violence, chaired by Sarah Brady. The Center is the nation's foremost organization working to reduce handgun violence in the United States through education, research, and legal action. The Center focuses strongly on reducing gun violence afflicting children, teens, and families. Two Center programs of note, among others, are:

- *Straight Talk About Risks (STAR):* STAR is a comprehensive gun violence prevention program for school and youth agencies, designed to teach children and teens problem-solving skills.

- *Steps to Prevent (STOP) Firearm Injury:* STOP was developed by the Center and the American Academy of Pediatrics to encourage health professionals to talk to parents about gun risks in the home and community.

For more information, please call or write:

Center to Prevent Handgun Violence
1225 Eye Street, N.W., #1100
Washington, D.C. 20005
(202) 289-7319

This book is dedicated to Kaitlyn, and to children everywhere,
with hopes for a more peaceful future.
—Q.L.P.

For Graham
—L.N.

Copyright © 1995 by RGA Publishing Group, Inc.
All rights reserved. No part of this work may be reproduced or transmitted in any form or by any means, electronic or mechanical, including photocopying and recording, or by any information storage or retrieval system, except as may be expressly permitted by the 1976 Copyright Act or in writing by the publisher.

Manufactured in the United States of America

ISBN: 1-56565-357-2

10 9 8 7 6 5 4 3 2 1

Publisher: Jack Artenstein
Vice President/General Manager, Juvenile Division: Elizabeth Amos
Director of Publishing Services: Rena Copperman
Editorial Director: Brenda Pope-Ostrow
Project Editor: Lisa Melton
Art Director: Lisa-Theresa Lenthall
Designer: Carolyn Wendt

Lowell House books can be purchased at special discounts when ordered in bulk for premiums and special sales. Contact Department JH at the following address:
Lowell House Juvenile
2029 Century Park East, Suite 3290
Los Angeles, CA 90067

Kid Talk

This is a book about guns and violence. Both can be very scary and very dangerous. Do you know what you should do if you see someone with a gun? Do you know what you can do to feel safe? This book will help you to answer these questions. This book also includes lots of fun activities that you can do at home with your friends and family. These activities will teach you a lot about guns and violence.

As you read through the pages, many questions you have about guns will be answered. If you have other questions that aren't answered, it's a good idea to talk to someone you trust about them. That might be an adult in your family, a teacher, a police officer, or any other adult you know.

Just remember, if you see a gun . . .

Chapter 1

What Is Violence?

When people talk about violence, what do they mean? Violence is when someone hurts another person or living thing on purpose—even himself or herself. Sometimes people can be very mean to each other. They do this by yelling, kicking, biting, calling names, hitting, or throwing things. Some people even use knives or guns to hurt others. Some people hurt other living things, too, such as animals. These are all different forms of violence.

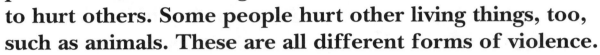

Hands On: Finger People

How does violence start? Usually, it starts with anger. When people get very angry, they might not care who gets hurt. Sometimes the best thing to do when *you* are angry is just turn and walk away. You can use these puppets to practice how you would act to avoid a fight. Pretend that your puppets are angry with each other and are about to fight. Think of ways they can solve the problem without fighting or hurting each other.

materials

- construction paper • marking pen
- scissors • tape • ruler

1 On construction paper, draw two figures (like those in the illustration) about 2 inches high. On each figure, draw in eyes, a mouth, and any other details you like. Now cut out both puppets.

2 Cut out two 2-inch-long and ½-inch-wide construction paper strips. Wrap each one around the tips of each of your index fingers to form rings. Tape the ends.

3 Tape one puppet to each ring. Now pretend that the puppets are arguing, and practice different ways to help them avoid a fight.

Working Together

1 What are your three favorite television shows?

Is it violent?

_____	_____ yes	_____ no
_____	_____ yes	_____ no
_____	_____ yes	_____ no

2 Is violence sometimes shown to make people laugh or as being funny on television? What do you think of that?

_____

3 How do you feel when someone yells or screams at you?

_____

Chapter 2

Finding a Better Way

Do you sometimes get angry? Being angry is O.K. Everyone feels angry at one time or another. What is important is how you show your anger. It is not O.K. to kick, hit, push, or use violence against someone else because you are upset. There are better ways to deal with your anger, such as seeking the help of a trusted adult. The kids in this picture are settling their differences by playing one-on-one basketball. Shooting hoops is one way of working off some anger energy. Can you think of another way to work off some anger?

_____

Hands On: "Feelings" Face

When you get angry at someone, do you feel like yelling at that person? Do you feel like hurting the person? When someone is angry at you, how do *you* feel? Do you get scared, or sad? Or do you get angry right back? Often, when someone is angry at you, it's hard to tell exactly what you are feeling. Drawing a picture or writing a story can help you understand what you're feeling.

Here's another way. You can use this special dough to make a "feelings" face.

materials

• 1 cup flour • ½ cup salt • 1 cup water • waxed paper
• bowl • toothpick or pencil

1 Mix the flour, salt, and water together in the bowl until you have a soft dough. If it feels sticky, add more flour. If it won't stay together, add water. Use this quiet time to think about what you are feeling.

2 Roll the dough into a ball and place it on the waxed paper. On one side of the ball, mold an angry face. You can use a toothpick, pencil, or even your fingertips to carve in any detail. On the other side of the ball, make a happy face.

3 Place your creation in a warm, sunny spot for several hours. This will dry out the dough, and your "feelings face" will last longer.

Working Together

1 On a separate piece of paper, write a story about the last time you were angry. In your story, tell why you were angry. Draw a picture to go with your story.

2 Write down two things that make you very angry.

_____   _____

3 What things can you do or say to feel better when you're angry?

_____

_____

_____

Chapter 3

Guns Are Not Toys

People sometimes get very angry or very frightened. When that happens, some people know how to deal with their anger or fear. They don't take it out on others by hurting them. But some people *don't* **know how to deal with their anger or fear. They might even think that guns can fix what's bothering them. One thing is certain: Guns are not toys. Guns can hurt you. People can die from gunshot wounds.**

Hands On: Nonviolent Vest

On television, you might see an actor pretend to be hurt or killed by someone with a gun. Later, you might see that same actor on another show and he will be all right. This is just pretend.

Real guns are not like the guns on television. They are not like toy guns, either. Real guns are dangerous. In real life, people who die from gunshot wounds do *not* get up later and walk away. Guns are not toys. If you see someone with a gun, choose to walk away to protect yourself. Life *should* be protected.

People who work hard to protect the lives of others, such as police officers, firefighters, and lifeguards, often wear special clothing with a marking, called an insignia, to identify themselves. Here's how to make a special nonviolent vest to identify yourself as a supporter of the "No Guns for Me" idea.

materials

• **brown paper grocery bag** • **scissors** • **colored markers**

1 Cut three holes in the grocery bag, one for your head at the top and two for your arms on the sides. Also cut a line up the center of the front of the bag, along the dotted line as shown. This is your vest.

2 Now draw on your "No Guns for Me" insignia and decorate the vest any way you like.

Working Together

1 Do you have any toy knives, guns, or toy soldiers? Describe some games that kids play with such toys. Are these games violent? Name a fun nonviolent game.

_____

_____

2 Sometimes soldiers and police officers help people who are in trouble, such as after a flood or an earthquake. Can you think of ways that soldiers might help disaster victims?

_____

_____

3 Even in times of danger, many people such as doctors and nurses, news reporters, ministers, priests, and rabbis do their jobs without the use of guns. Describe the jobs each of these people do. Do you think these people are brave? Write your answers on a separate piece of paper.

Chapter 4

Another Point of View

It is sometimes necessary for some people to carry guns. You shouldn't be afraid if you see a police officer, security guard, or a soldier with a gun. It is part of their job to carry a gun. They have been trained to use it carefully and safely. They are working hard to keep our homes and neighborhoods safe.

Hands On: Good News Journal

If you watch the news on television, or listen to it on the radio, it might seem as if the world is filled with violence. It might seem very scary. When you feel afraid, talk about your fear with an adult you trust, such as a parent or teacher.

It's also fun to look for the *good* things that are happening in your neighborhood, and to notice the people working to make the world a safer place. Why not keep a journal of good news? In it you could write down things that people in your town are doing to help stop violence. Here's how to make a special cover, called a collage, for your journal.

materials

- **magazines and newspapers • scissors • construction paper • white glue**
- **wide paintbrush • 12 inches of yarn • pen or pencil • small bowl • water**
- **several sheets of notebook paper • stapler**

1 You will need two 8½-by-11-inch sheets of construction paper. These will be the front and back covers of your Good News Journal. Write "GOOD NEWS JOURNAL" as shown.

2 Begin by looking through the magazines and newspapers for pictures of people doing good deeds or having fun together. Cut out enough pictures to cover the front and back covers of the notebook you'll make.

3 Place the notebook covers on a flat surface. Glue the pictures you have chosen in place. It's O.K. to overlap some of them if you like.

4 Place a tablespoon of glue in the bowl and mix in about ½ tablespoon of water. Use a wide brush to coat your collage with a light layer of the mixture.

11

5 When the covers are dry, staple them together with several sheets of notebook paper in between. You can also use yarn to tie your pencil to the top of your notebook.

Working Together

1 Why do you think police officers, security guards, and soldiers carry guns?

_____

_____

Would police need guns if there were no shootings or crimes with guns?

_____

2 Write a story about a make-believe land in which there are no guns. Give your make-believe land a name, and tell what life is like there without guns. Is there war in your make-believe land? If there isn't, how do people settle differences? Draw a picture to go with your story. Continue your story on a separate piece of paper.

_____

_____

_____

_____

_____

_____

_____

No-Violence Zone

School is a place to learn. It is easier to study and learn when you feel comfortable and safe. Guns don't belong in school, unless they're carried by visiting police officers. If you see someone with a gun in or near your school, tell your teacher right away. Be smart! Stay away from guns.

Hands On: Safe Haven

You don't spend your whole school day in your classroom. You spend some of the time walking or riding to and from school. You also have a special time for lunch, and a special time to play on the playground. Kids might get into fights during those times. That might make you feel scared or angry. Some kids might even pull out a gun.

But school is a "no-violence" zone. It's supposed to be a safe place, and your teachers want you to feel safe. If someone tries to start a fight with you, or if you see others fighting, let your teacher know. Help keep your school safe inside and out. Here's a way to have fun while you're outside. This bird feeder does two jobs at once. It gives the birds a safe place to eat, and it gives you a chance to have fun peacefully watching them.

materials

• 1 empty half-gallon milk carton • 3 feet of heavy string • Popsicle stick
• scissors • birdseed or popped popcorn

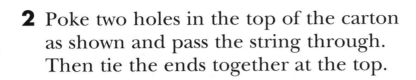

1 Rinse the milk carton. Cut a large hole out of one side, leaving a slight overhang on the top and a lip on the bottom about 1½ inches deep as shown. Paste a Popsicle stick on the lower lip to give the birds a place to land.

2 Poke two holes in the top of the carton as shown and pass the string through. Then tie the ends together at the top.

3 Fill the bottom of the feeder with seed or popcorn, and hang it in a place where the birds will be safe from hunting cats. Now you can spend peaceful, quiet time watching the birds and feel good about caring for other living things.

Working Together

1 What are some things you like about school?

_____

_____

2 What are some of the things you think *belong* in school?

_____

_____

Do guns belong in school? _____

What would you do if you saw someone with a gun in school?

_____

_____

Play It Safe

Some people keep guns in their homes. These guns are not toys! If an adult in your family has a gun, do not touch it. If you see your brother or sister or a friend pick up a gun, move away and tell them to put it down. Then tell an adult you trust what happened.

Remember, guns can hurt you!

Hands On: Friendship Mobile

Guns in the home should be locked in a safe place. They should not be loaded with bullets. These are rules of safety. But not all adults follow these rules.

If you are at a friend's house and your friend wants to show you a gun, say NO! Even if your friend says the gun is not loaded, you can't be sure of that. If your friend picks up the gun, move away and tell him or her to put it down. Then go and tell an adult, such as your mom or dad, what happened.

Take some time to think about the people you trust. They might be your parents, teachers, grandparents, neighbors, or someone else. You can keep these people in your thoughts by making a friendship mobile. Each mobile will hold five pictures you draw. If you have photos, use those instead.

materials

- **2 plastic drinking straws • string • tape • glue**
- **heavy white poster board • colored marking pens**
- **photographs or drawings • scissors**

1 Ask each of five trusted adults for a snapshot of themselves. If they don't have one, draw a picture. Trim each picture into a 2- or 3-inch-square size.

2 Cut out a square piece of poster board for each picture, large enough to leave at least a ¼-inch "frame" around the photo. Glue the photo to the center of the board, then write the person's name and phone number at the base of the frame. Draw designs on the rest of the frame. Punch a small hole in the top of each frame and tie a piece of string, about 6 inches long, through each hole.

3 Now it's time to make the hanger that will hold your pictures. Cross two straws to make an X as shown, then cross strips of tape at the center so the straws stay in place. Tie one end of a 12-inch piece of string in the center of the X, and make a small loop at the other end. This is your hanger.

4 Using the scissors, snip a small slit in both ends of each straw. Slip the loose end of the string on one photo frame into one slit, then tie it securely as shown. Repeat this at each corner. Tie the fifth photo frame to the center of the X.

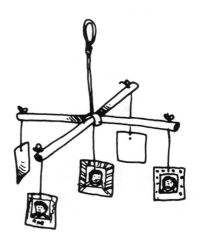

Working Together

1 Why do some people want a gun in their home?

_____

_____

Besides owning a gun, are there other things people could do to feel safe?

_____

_____

2 Write a list of the five adults you chose to be on your friendship mobile. Next to each name, write down why you trust that person.

Name	Why do you trust him or her?
_____	_____
_____	_____
_____	_____
_____	_____
_____	_____

Street Safety

Guns are dangerous. Innocent people can be hurt by guns. If you see someone on the street with a gun, run the other way. Find an adult you trust and tell him or her what you saw. If you happen to hear gunshots while you are outside, stay calm. Go inside your home, school, or other safe place as quickly as possible, move away from the windows, and stay down.

Hands On: Fun Phone

Some neighborhoods are quiet and peaceful. You might never hear a gunshot, and people are rarely hurt. Other neighborhoods are violent and dangerous. Sometimes gang members fight openly in the streets, and it is hard to feel safe. Still other neighborhoods are somewhere in between. But in every neighborhood, there are places you can call—or where you can go—to feel safe. Make a list of such places. The list might include your school, your church, a recreation center, the police station, or a neighbor's house. Write down the telephone numbers of your safe places, and keep the list near the phone at home. Make a copy to keep in your school notebook. Here's how to make a "short range" fun phone so you and a friend can call each other.

materials

• **2 paper drinking cups** • **20 feet of twine** • **2 toothpicks** • **scissors**

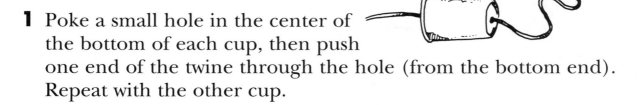

1 Poke a small hole in the center of the bottom of each cup, then push one end of the twine through the hole (from the bottom end). Repeat with the other cup.

2 Now snap off the ends of the toothpicks. Tie both ends of the twine in a tight knot around a toothpick as shown. Pull gently on the twine coming from the bottom of the cup. The toothpick will prevent the twine from coming out.

3 To use your phone with a friend, stand far enough apart so that the twine is straight and tight. Speak softly into the open end of your cup, while your friend listens to the open end of the other cup. Why not use your fun phone to pretend to call one of your "safe places" from your phone list? For example, practice what you might say if you needed to call the police department.

Working Together

1 You and a friend can each make a map of the "safe places" in your neighborhood. What will you put on *your* map?

_____ _____

_____ _____

_____ _____

2 How would you choose which place to go to if you saw someone in the street with a gun?

_____

_____

Chapter 8

Everyone Counts

Sometimes people carry guns because they think it makes them look tough or strong. Sometimes these people even use the guns against others. But hurting innocent people does not make them tough and strong. It makes them mean and violent. It is sad when people get hurt. Every day, people die from gunshot wounds. When a gun is used to injure or kill, many people feel the pain.

Hands On: Dream Catcher

Do you know what you want to be when you grow up? All of the doctors, scientists, police officers, astronauts, firefighters, and teachers you see and hear about today were once children with special dreams. Someday, the children of today will take their place in the grown-up world, too.

Do you have a dream for your future? Here is how to make a Dream Catcher. Native Americans say that the strings in a Dream Catcher snare bad dreams so they won't trouble your sleep. Only good dreams slip through!

materials

• 2 feet of aluminum foil • 1 ball of yarn or colored string
• scissors • plastic beads or dry tube pasta

1 Twist about two feet of aluminum foil into a long tube shape, then bend it into a circle. Twist the ends so they stay together.

2 Tie one end of the yarn to the aluminum hoop, then loop the yarn around and around until the hoop is completely covered. When you're done, cut and tie off the end of the yarn.

3 Cut a piece of yarn about a foot long, then place it across the hoop and tie at each end. Cut another piece and do the same, leaving a gap of about an inch between the first and second knots. Do this until you have gone all the way around the hoop, then trim all the loose ends of yarn.

4 Tie both ends of a one-foot piece of yarn to the top of the hoop to make a hanger. To decorate your Dream Catcher, cut several 6-inch lengths of yarn and knot a plastic bead or piece of pasta at each end. Then tie them to the bottom of the hoop to make a fringe, and at the center, too.

Working Together

1 What would you like to be when you grow up?

_____

2 When you have your own home someday, what will it be like? Who will you want to live in your home with you?

_____

_____

It's Good to Be Me

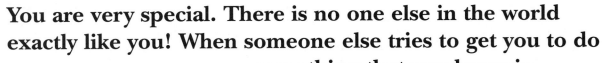

You are very special. There is no one else in the world exactly like you! When someone else tries to get you to do something that you know is wrong, you do not have to do it. If a friend wants you to play with a gun, you can say no, walk away, and do something else instead. You and your friends can always find fun things to do that are *safe* and *smart*.

Hands On: "It's Me!" Portrait

Sometimes friends might ask you to do things that you know you really shouldn't do. When that happens, do you ever go along just to please your friends? Do you feel that they won't like you if you say no? Sometimes it's hard to say no to your friends. But you know what is best for you. You are your own best friend. You are special. Here's a way to make a frame for a picture of a wonderful person—YOU!

materials

• a picture of you (a photo, or a picture you've drawn yourself, about 2 or 3 inches square) • heavy poster board • ruler
• marking pen • scissors • glue • string • dried pasta shells
• poster paint or glitter (optional)

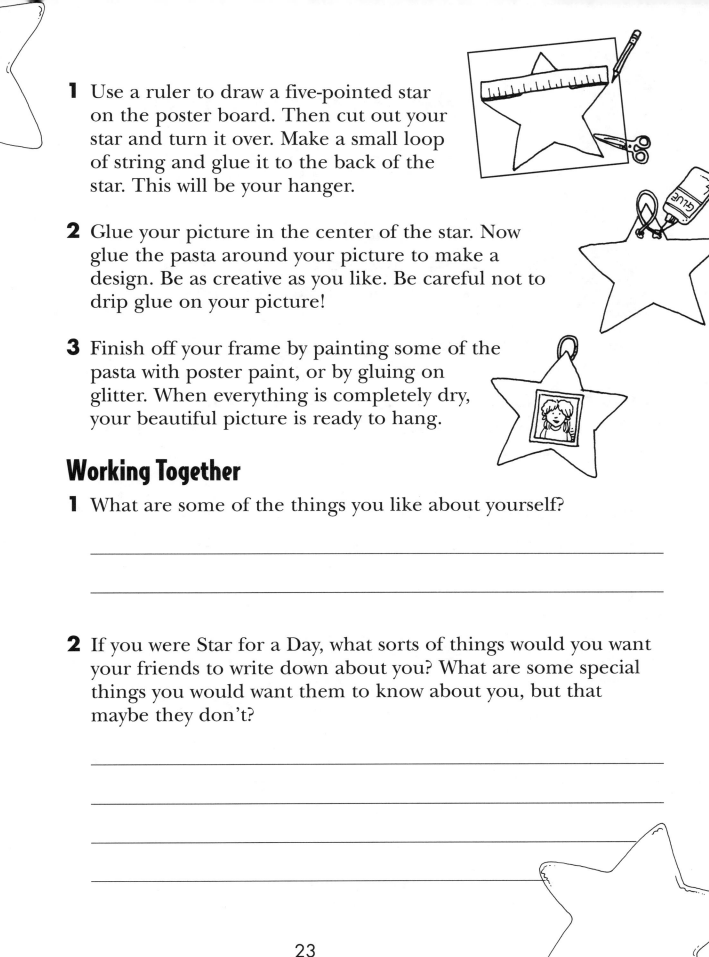

1 Use a ruler to draw a five-pointed star on the poster board. Then cut out your star and turn it over. Make a small loop of string and glue it to the back of the star. This will be your hanger.

2 Glue your picture in the center of the star. Now glue the pasta around your picture to make a design. Be as creative as you like. Be careful not to drip glue on your picture!

3 Finish off your frame by painting some of the pasta with poster paint, or by gluing on glitter. When everything is completely dry, your beautiful picture is ready to hang.

Working Together

1 What are some of the things you like about yourself?

_____

_____

2 If you were Star for a Day, what sorts of things would you want your friends to write down about you? What are some special things you would want them to know about you, but that maybe they don't?

_____

_____

_____

_____

My Place in the Community

You might think that grown-ups don't pay a lot of attention to kids. That might be true of some grown-ups, but most of them think kids are a really important part of the community, and they want to help you whenever you need it. If you see someone with a gun, or if you hear gunshots, find an adult you trust and tell him or her what happened. They are there to listen and help.

Hands On: Puzzle Time

You are important, and no one else can fill your place. To begin with, you are a part of your family. And no other family is exactly like yours. You might have lots of brothers and sisters, or none at all. You might have one parent, two parents, or perhaps grandparents taking care of you. You might have an adoptive family, or you may live with a foster family.

You play many other roles in the community, too. You are a neighbor, a student in a class, perhaps a member of a church or a synagogue, or on a sports team, or in a choir. Here's something fun to do while you are thinking about your special place in the community: turn it into a puzzle!

materials

• heavy poster board (at least 8½ by 11 inches in size) • marking pen
• crayons or colored pencils • scissors

1 On heavy poster board, draw a detailed map of your neighborhood.

2 Use the crayons or pencils to color your map. Put a star on each place in the map that you feel you belong to. These are *your* places in the community! Then draw some heavy lines to create a grid pattern on the map.

3 Cut along all of the heavy lines to create individual puzzle pieces. Then mix up the pieces and try to put your puzzle together again. As you will find, every piece is important to make your neighborhood complete.

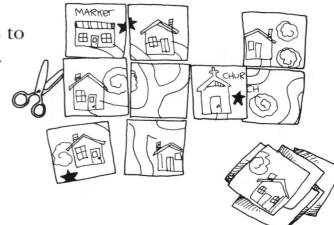

Working Together

1 Draw a big picture of a neighborhood tree. Draw a picture of yourself in the center of the tree and add lines above and below your picture. On the lines, fill in the names of friends, family members, pets, neighbors—anyone you care about.

2 Do you know what your place is at home? In what ways do you help out?

_____

_____

How about at school? Do you do special things for your school that only a kid could do?

_____

_____

Chapter 11

Feelings

Have you ever been to a movie that really *scared* you? Has anything ever happened at home or school that made you feel very *sad*? Do you get *angry* sometimes? *Scared*, *sad*, and *angry* are all feelings, and it's O.K. to feel all of those things. Everybody does. The important thing is how you choose to show your feelings. Using a gun if you are angry, sad, or afraid is not a good choice.

Hands On: Patient Puppy

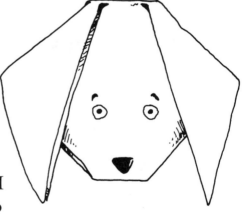

It isn't always easy to control your feelings, and sometimes you shouldn't have to. It's O.K. to cry if you are sad, or to yell out if something scares you. But the best thing to do when you are angry is to think about what has made you angry. Ask yourself: What am I feeling? Why am I angry? What are my choices about what to do? Some choices are better than others. When you are ready, talk calmly and honestly to someone about your feelings. The best person to talk to may be the one who made you angry.

It's good to practice what you might say to someone you're angry at. You can try that out on this patient puppy. It's made by using the ancient oriental art of paper folding, called origami.

materials

• 2 pieces of paper (any color or pattern), cut into squares that are 4 inches long on each side • 2 small buttons • glue • marker

1 Begin by folding a square piece of paper into a triangle. Work slowly and carefully, 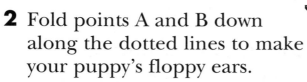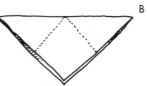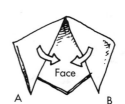 making your fold crisp and neat. You can take this quiet time to think about how you are feeling.

2 Fold points A and B down along the dotted lines to make your puppy's floppy ears.

A   B

Face

A   B

3 Then fold over the top and bottom corners— away from the face—to give the head the proper shape.

4 Use a marker to draw on the pup's nose and mouth. Glue buttons in place for eyes. You can color your puppy if you like. The finished design looks cute glued on a notebook!

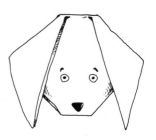

Working Together

1 Why do you suppose it is better when you are angry to stop and think before you act?

_____

_____

2 Have you ever been angry at someone only to find out later that the person was not at fault? How do you think false rumors get started? What would you do to stop the spread of a rumor?

_____

_____

_____

Chapter 12

Feeling Scared

Sometimes it's fun to get a little scared. Maybe you like spooky stories, or you like to dress up in something scary for Halloween. That's O.K. What *isn't* O.K. or fun is to be afraid of getting hurt. Violence can be very scary. Guns are dangerous. It's best to just stay away from them.

Hands On: Monster Masks

Everyone is afraid of something. Some people don't like to ride in elevators or go up in tall buildings. Some people are afraid of flying in airplanes, or of thunderstorms. Some people don't like spiders or snakes. Ask your family and friends what they are afraid of. You might be surprised at some of the answers. That's because we're not all afraid of the same things.

It's natural to be scared sometimes. If you are afraid of something in particular, it can help you to draw a picture of what you fear or to write a story about it. Then show your picture or story to someone you trust and talk about your feelings. And don't forget, some things can be scary, but safe and fun, too— such as amusement park rides, scary movies, and Halloween masks. Just for fun, here's how to make a mask that can be as scary as you like.

materials

• brown paper grocery bag • felt-tip markers • glue • scissors
• tape • scraps of fabric and yarn • dry, uncooked macaroni

1 Using a pair of scissors, shorten a brown paper bag so that it fits comfortably over your head. Put it on, then find the spots on the bag where you will need eye holes (you'll have to do this by feel). Mark these places with a felt-tip pen.

2 Take the bag off and cut out the eye holes. Now it's time to make your bag scary! You might draw the face of a fierce dinosaur or a scary space monster with three eyes. Use yarn or fabric for hair. Dry macaroni can be curved teeth. Be creative!

Working Together

1 Do some things frighten you? What are these things, and why do you suppose they scare you? Make a list.

What scares you?   *Why* does it scare you?

_____   _____

_____   _____

_____   _____

_____   _____

2 Ask a friend to help you make up a scary story! Write the story on a separate piece of paper. Be sure to draw a picture to go with the story. If you draw one of the story's characters, be sure to write down his or her name, too.

Feeling Safe

Some people think that having a gun around will keep them safe. But guns are dangerous. It is *never* safe to play with a gun, even if someone tells you it is not loaded. Be smart. Leave guns alone.

Hands On: Marvelous Maze

There are things that can be both safe *and* dangerous. Medicine can help to make you better. But you should never take any drugs or medicine unless your doctor or your parents give it to you. Matches can start a warm fire, but fires can get out of hand, burning down homes and hurting people. Police officers are trained to handle guns safely. But in the wrong hands, guns are *very dangerous.*

Make this maze, and you can lead a friend from danger to safety.

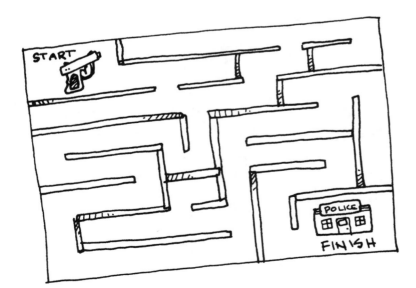

materials

• 1 piece each of red and green construction paper
• paste or glue • marker • button • scissors

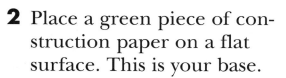

1 Cut one piece of red construction paper lengthwise in ½-inch-wide strips.

2 Place a green piece of construction paper on a flat surface. This is your base. Now paste red construction paper strips to the base to create your maze. You can copy one of the mazes shown, or make up your own. Draw a gun at the start of the maze and put a "police station" sign at the finish.

3 Use a button to represent a child who has just seen someone with a gun. Guide the child through the maze from danger to safety.

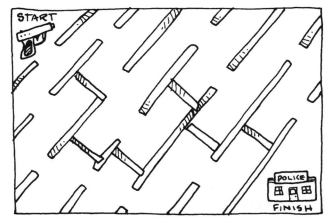

31

Working Together

1 Make a list of some of the things that protect you and make you feel safe. Why do these things make you feel safe?

What makes you feel safe?   *Why* does it make you feel safe?

_____   _____

_____

_____   _____

_____

_____   _____

2 If you had to, you could get through a dark forest all by yourself! What are some things you would need to do that?

_____

_____

_____

3 What word means "safe" to you?

_____

If you could draw a picture of this word, what would it look like? Draw your picture on a separate piece of paper.

Chapter 14

Getting in Touch with Feelings

Your feelings are your own. No one else can tell you *what* to feel or *how* to feel. Sometimes you might get confused and not understand your feelings. You might feel afraid, or sad, or upset  **without knowing why. How would you feel if you saw someone on the street with a gun? What would you do?**

Hands On: Making Music

Have you ever broken something by accident, such as a dish? If so, you might have felt a lot of different feelings all at once. You might have been angry that the dish was broken. Maybe you were afraid, too, because you thought someone would get angry at you. Maybe you were sad to have broken the dish. You might have even felt good because you wanted to do something to hurt someone. It isn't always easy to understand your own feelings, especially when they're jumbled up together. But you're not alone. Everyone gets confused sometimes. That's why it is good to talk to someone. Talking will help you to understand and "get in touch with" your feelings.

When you *don't* feel like talking to anybody, or there's no one around to talk to, music can help you to work through your feelings, too. Here's how to make your own "instrument."

materials

- • 1 half-gallon milk carton • 2 Popsicle sticks
- • 4 long rubber bands of different thicknesses
- • scissors

1 To make your own guitar, cut a 2-inch hole in the front of the milk carton about halfway up. Glue one Popsicle stick across the bottom of the hole and one across the top as shown.

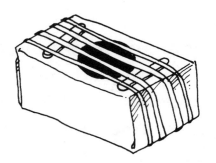

2 Now stretch each of the rubber bands around the milk carton, lengthwise, starting with the thickest one. Leave a little room between each rubber band. Now strum your "guitar." If the sound is dull, raise the "strings" by gluing another Popsicle stick on top of each of the first ones. Now you are ready to express your feelings through music!

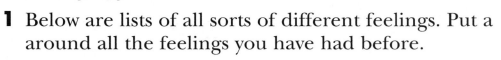

Working Together

1 Below are lists of all sorts of different feelings. Put a ◯ around all the feelings you have had before.

hot	**cold**	**wet**	**tired**
hungry	**thirsty**	**happy**	**angry**
hurt	**sad**	**afraid**	**mean**

Now put a ☐ around the feelings you think you might have if you saw a gun.

2 Play some of your favorite music. How did the music make you feel? Try to draw a picture of that feeling.

3 *Playing music* is one way of expressing your feelings. *Listening to music* and *dancing to music* are other ways. Can you think of two other ways to show others how you're feeling? Write them down.

_____

_____

Chapter 15

Caring

One way to stop violence is to care about each other. Our schools and neighborhoods will be safer if we all take time to care for one another. If you see someone with a gun, do your part to protect your friends and neighbors. Find a parent or other grown-up, a teacher, or a police officer and tell that person what you saw. Or, call the national emergency number, 9-1-1.

Hands On: Double Duty

It feels good when you do something nice for another person or another living thing. If you have a dog, you know how nice it feels when you give your furry pal a treat and see his or her tail wag happily. It feels good when a friend or family member thanks you for something nice you have done.

Here's a way you can make a keepsake bowl to hold special treasures, such as snapshots or mementos of fun times you have spent with someone you care about. It's even a way you can do something nice for planet Earth, because this papier-mâché bowl is made from old newspaper! Recycling used paper means less garbage, and it's a way to show others you care!

materials

• ½ cup of flour • ⅔ cup of water • bowl • plenty of old newspaper
• vegetable oil • 1 round balloon • poster paint • paintbrush
• paper towel (or napkin)

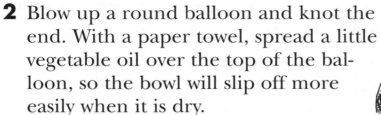

1 In a bowl or plastic container, mix ½ cup flour and ⅔ cup water to make a paste. Now tear the newspaper into long, thin strips.

2 Blow up a round balloon and knot the end. With a paper towel, spread a little vegetable oil over the top of the balloon, so the bowl will slip off more easily when it is dry.

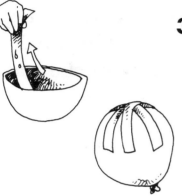

3 Dip strips of paper one by one into the paste. Allow the strip to drip a little, then place it over the balloon "form." Keep adding paper until you have completed your bowl. Let dry for 24 hours, then pop the balloon and remove it. If you like, you can paint your bowl with poster paints.

Working Together

1 Do you know what it means to be a leader? What are some of the responsibilities a leader must take? Blindfold a friend and lead him or her around your room. How did it feel to be a leader? Now have your friend lead you around the room. How did it feel to be led while blindfolded?

_____

_____

_____

2 How does it make you feel when someone else takes care of you when you are sick?

_____

Chapter 16

Getting to Know You

Friends come in all sizes, colors, and ages. The best way to *make* a friend is to *be* a friend. By being a good listener when someone is afraid or unhappy, you are being a friend. When you keep someone safe from violence or warn them about something dangerous, you are also being a good friend. What would you do if a friend told you he or she had a gun?

GUNS AREN'T TOYS. THEY'RE VERY DANGEROUS!

_____

_____

Hands On: Friendship Notes

When you don't know someone very well, you might have a wrong idea about that person. You might think they're unfriendly, but when you get to know them better, you find out they're just shy. It's *never* a good idea to judge people just on how they look, or where they are from. It's *always* a good idea to give people a chance before you make up your mind about them. Here's a way to let a couple of people get to know *you*— by making them each a friendship note.

DEAR SAM,
TELL YOU
LIKE TO
PIANO?
WRITE
LET IT
TO GO.

materials

• construction paper • several old kitchen sponges • scissors
• aluminum foil • poster paint • paintbrush • paper towels

1 Cut small sponges into different shapes as shown.

2 Your card can be any size you like, but an 8½-by-11-inch sheet of paper works well for making two cards. Fold the sheet lengthwise, then cut it in half as shown. You will get two blank cards.

3 Pour a small pool of poster paint onto a piece of aluminum foil. Dip one of the shaped sponges into the paint, then blot it lightly on a paper towel. Now use the sponge to make a paint imprint on the front of your card.

4 Continue making imprints on both your cards until you are happy with the designs. Use as many colors as you like. When the paint is dry, you can write a message inside. Write things that will help the person get to know who you are! List your favorite qualities about yourself, and why you think you're special.

Working Together

1 Draw a picture of a close friend of yours. On a separate piece of paper, write a story about that friend. Include things like what your friend likes to do for fun, and what sort of family he or she has.

2 People celebrate holidays and other events in many different ways. Pick two events or holidays and describe how you celebrate them in your own family. Ask a friend to do the same thing, but about his or her own family. Are there any differences? Are there any similarities? Write your answers on a separate piece of paper.

Teamwork

It's easier to do a good job when everyone works on the job together. Sometimes people don't agree on how things should be done. That's O.K., because we can't always agree on everything. But it's *not* O.K. to use violence to settle disagreements. Some people think that by using a gun they will get their way. But using a gun will only make things worse.

Hands On: Picture Parts

Everyone is different, and everyone has his or her own special way of doing things. When you disagree with someone, it is important to talk about your differences. It is important to find a solution that everyone can accept. That is called a compromise. Here's a fun game to play at parties, with an equal number of friends, that requires teamwork to succeed.

materials

- **one magazine picture of an animal for every player (the pictures should be cut evenly into thirds) • box • construction paper • marking pen • glue**

1 Ask a grown-up to cut the animal pictures into thirds and place them in a box. You and your friends must pick a section of a magazine picture of an animal from the box. You each have to find the other two friends who have the parts that go with yours.

2 Once you have found each other, you and your team must glue each picture part to a single piece of construction paper to make a complete picture. Now identify the animal and write its name on the bottom of the paper.

3 The first team to finish its picture and cross a finish line that a grown-up has set up wins.

Working Together

1 Circle the answer below that you think would be the most important step toward settling an argument between two friends. Write down why you chose the answer you did.

    a Listen to both sides of the story.
    b Do not yell or shout.
    c Ask each person for an opinion on what would be a fair solution.
    d Have your friends shake hands.

2 Imagine that someone has just shown you a pretty flowering plant. If you and a friend both want the plant, how can that happen without hurting it? Write your answer on a separate piece of paper.

Working Together

Sometimes it's scary to stand up for what you believe in. It's easier if you have the support of friends. Let your friends know how you feel about guns and violence. You might be surprised to find that they feel the same way.

DO YOU THINK GUNS ARE DANGEROUS?

GUNS CAN KILL YOU!

Hands On: Fun and Games

Getting together with your friends can be lots of fun. It's especially fun when everyone tries to get along well. That is called cooperation. Some people don't want to cooperate, or they don't know how. Some people might use violence, or even a gun, to get their own way. When that happens, concerned members of the community can cooperate with police officers to help stop the violence.

Here are a couple of games you can play with your friends that require lots of cooperation.

materials

• several pieces of ribbon, each about 3 feet long, or several scarves
• 2 basketballs • 2 empty trash cans • watch

1 The first game is the three-legged obstacle course. You can play this on the playground at school, in your backyard, or in a park. You'll need at least four players, but you can have as many as you want. Have everyone pick a partner.

Agree on an obstacle course that includes things to step over and climb under. Have partners stand side by side, and then tie their inner legs together with ribbon or a scarf. Now see which team can finish the course fastest. It will take a lot of cooperation between partners to win!

2 For tummy basketball, set up two trash cans about 10 feet apart. Have each pair of partners start about 30 feet from the cans. The object is to see which team can race down the "court" first and sink a basket. The catch is that they cannot touch the ball with their hands. Facing each other with their hands behind their backs, the partners must hold up the ball between their tummies.

Working Together

1 If you had a big job to do, why would it be easier or faster to have the help of a couple of friends?

_____

_____

2 How do you think community members can help police officers to stop neighborhood violence? What can *you* do to help?

_____

_____

Chapter 19 Kid Power

You might feel that there isn't much you can do to help stop violence. But there is. In fact, you can do a lot! You are helping just by making the choice not to use violence. When you decide that you won't argue with someone, won't call them names or hit them, and won't play with guns, you are taking a step toward making a better world. You've got kid power!

Hands On: Power on the Line

What is kid power? It's the ability to get things done, even against tough odds. In 1980, the fourth grade students at McElwain Elementary School in Colorado decided they wanted *Stegosaurus* to be their state dinosaur. They wrote letters, visited the state capitol, and talked to reporters. In 1982, *Stegosaurus* was named the state dinosaur of Colorado. That's kid power!

Kids have even used kid power to save friends' or family members' lives by calling the national emergency number, 9-1-1. You and your friends can use these directions to practice how to make a call in case of an emergency. Your mom or dad can pretend to be the operator.

materials

- **a toy phone, drawing of a phone, or picture of a phone pad**
- **a list of emergency situations to act out**

1 It is very important to remember that 9-1-1 is a special number that should be used *only* in emergencies. Find the numbers 9-1-1 on a toy phone or on a drawing of a telephone. Punch in the numbers and wait for the operator to answer. Then tell him or her what the problem is and answer all questions clearly and calmly. Stay on the line and follow the instructions you are given.

2 Here are some of the questions that an operator might ask:

What is your name?	Who is hurt?
What is your address?	How old are you?
What has happened?	Is there anyone else in the house?

Working Together

1 Kids around the nation are using kid power to help solve the problems of pollution by conserving energy. What are two ways you can conserve electricity?

_____   _____

2 If you saw someone at the park with a gun, what are two ways you could use kid power to prevent someone from getting hurt?

_____   _____

3 What are two ways that you and your friends can use kid power to help stop violence in your community?

_____   _____

Chapter 20

No Guns for Me!

Each and every day, you make lots of decisions all by yourself. When it comes to guns and violence, no one can make up your mind for you. You have to choose what you will do. If someone asked you to play with a gun, what would you do? When it comes to guns, the right choice is:

DON'T TOUCH IT.
MOVE AWAY FROM IT.
FIND HELP!

Hands On: Sticker Time

Guns and violence can cause pain and injury. Guns and violence are never a good choice. You can let everyone know that you have made the right choice by working for a better, safer, violence-free community.

To show your support for nonviolence, you can make your own "No Guns" notebook stickers. Here's how.

materials

• heavy white paper • crayons or colored pencils
• clear Con-Tact shelf paper • scissors

1 Design and color your sticker on a piece of heavy white paper. One design is shown on page 46, and one is shown here.

2 Cut out your drawing in a square, circle, triangle, star, or any other shape you prefer.

3 Place your drawing on top of the clear side of the Con-Tact paper and trace a circle a little larger than the drawing itself.

4 Figure out what clean surface you want to put your sticker on (a notebook? a lunch box?) and place your drawing there. Remove the backing from the Con-Tact paper and center the clear piece, sticky side down, over your drawing. Now stick it down and smooth the edges.

Working Together

1 Now that you have almost finished your activity book, do you feel differently about guns than when you started? If you do, write down how your feelings have changed.

_____

_____

2 If you had a chance to give a message to kids all over the world about guns, what would that message be?

_____

_____

NO GUNS FOR ME!

I _____ pledge to do my part to make

Child's Name

my neighborhood and school safer places. If I see

a gun, I will remember that the right choice is:

DON'T TOUCH IT.
MOVE AWAY FROM IT.
FIND HELP!

_____
Child's Signature

_____
Parent's Signature